LIGHT & SHADOW

by Myra Cohn Livingston

photographs by Barbara Rogasky

Holiday House / New York

For
JAKOB ROELAND BRUGGE,
whose light obliterates the shadows
M.C.L.
To the memory of
RALPH STEINER
(with appropriate nod and wink)
B.R.

Text copyright © 1992 by Myra Cohn Livingston
Photographs copyright © 1992 by Barbara Rogasky
PRINTED IN THE UNITED STATES OF AMERICA
First Edition

Library of Congress Cataloging-in-Publication Data
Livingston, Myra Cohn.
Light & Shadow / by Myra Cohn Livingston ;
photographs by Barbara Rogasky.
p.   cm.
Summary: A collection of 14 poems exploring the
changing nature of light.
ISBN 0-8234-0931-7
1. Children's poetry, American.   [1. Light—Poetry.
2. American poetry.]
I. Rogasky, Barbara, ill.   II. Title.
PS3562.I945L58   1992   91-22355   CIP   AC
811'.54—dc20

CONTENTS

DAYLIGHT
[4]

FROM AN AIRPLANE
[6]

TOLL BRIDGE
[8]

OCEAN
[10]

DINER
[12]

ABANDONED HOUSE
[14]

NEIGHBORHOOD STREETS
[16]

COUNTY FAIR
[18]

STREAM
[20]

CAMP
[22]

SHADOWS
[24]

LATE AFTERNOON
[26]

FAMILY ROOM
[28]

2 A.M.
[30]

DAYLIGHT

Light jumps
out of gray dawn
pushing a yellow ball
over

patches
of earth and sea,
shoving it higher than
city

buildings,
higher than the
tallest of all mountains
where it

slowly
circles the earth,
exploding the sky with
color.

FROM AN AIRPLANE

Light pins
on diamonds
and sapphires, wears bracelets
wound with

rubies
and emeralds;
buckles on studded belts
and drops

her rings,
bright necklaces,
dribbling silver and gold
over

the earth,
scattered bits of
baubles and beads, brightening
the night.

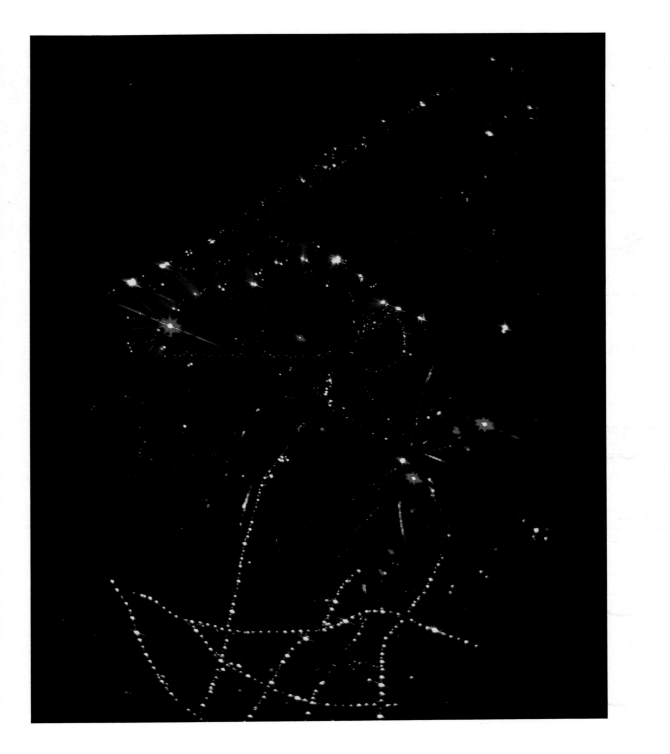

TOLL BRIDGE

Light is
a tolltaker,
a bridgemaster flashing
yellow

commands
to slow down, halt,
line up and wait in line
while blue

sentries
scoop into mesh
baskets the silver coins
thrown from

open
windows, and gate
arms rise up, leading to
darkness.

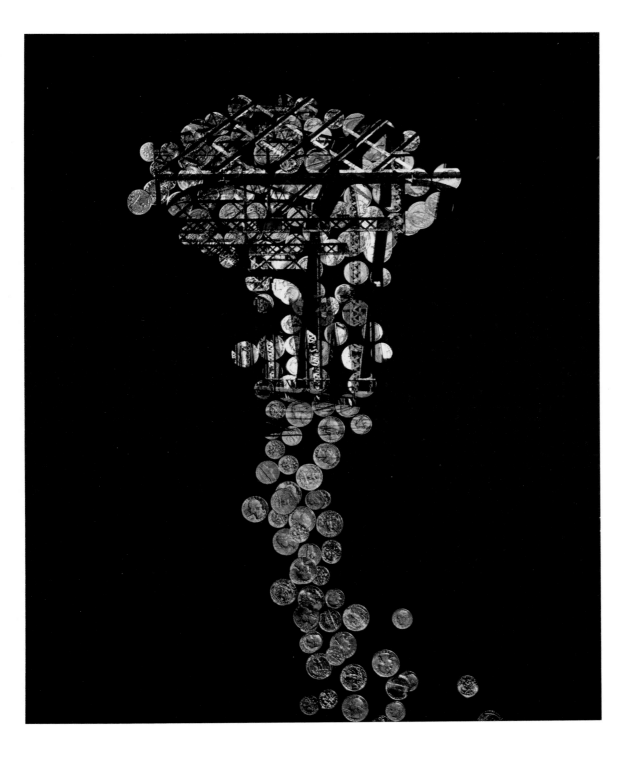

OCEAN

Light swims
in the ocean
tipping broken half-moons
over

the waves,
bobbing circles
into floating seaweed
near the

distant
horizon; then
climbs from the darkling shore
to dry

off in
the flickering
curve of a far-off beach
city.

DINER

Light is
waiting at a
street corner, watching for
blinking

arrows,
for red lights to
turn to yellow and green,
ready

to walk
across the street
to windows where BREAKFAST
AND HOT

DISHES,
PIZZA and HOT
PASTA signs all bloom in
neon.

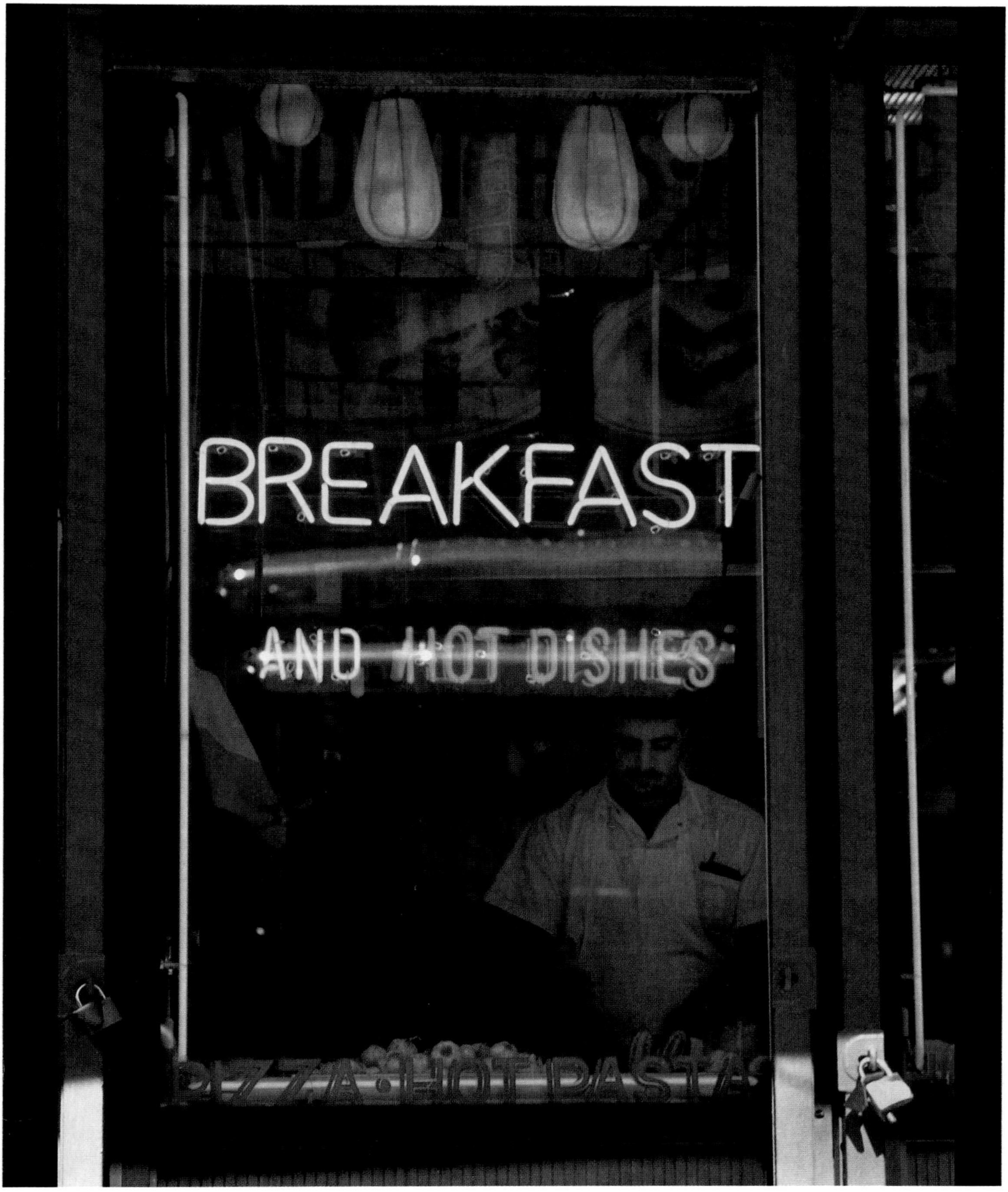
BREAKFAST
AND HOT DISHES

ABANDONED HOUSE

Light finds
a place to rest
on peeling windowsills,
lazes

among
branches of a
towering tree caught in
white sky,

peers through
a smoky pane
to a rippling curtain
and stares,

transfixed,
beyond broken
glass, to ghostly, floating
circles.

NEIGHBORHOOD STREETS

Light is
skittering on
quiet neighborhood streets,
stopping

to swing
from tall lampposts,
climbing into treetops,
arcing

over
sleeping grasses,
waiting on dark porches
for drawn

curtains
to part, shades to
rise, and front doors to swing
open.

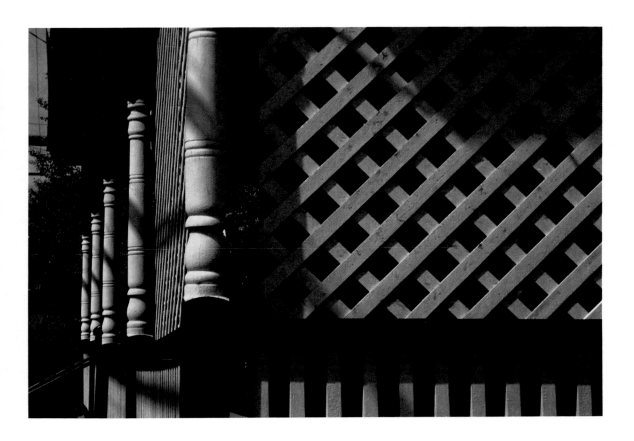

COUNTY FAIR

Light buys
a ticket to
the County Fair, spins in
circles

on a
merry-go-round,
spirals high on a
ferris

wheel, loops
the loops of a
giant roller coaster,
and laughs

at its
own reflection
bouncing in the Hall of
Mirrors.

STREAM

Light steps
into a pool,
stretching its yellow legs
deep down

into
a black mirror,
touching the bottom with
a cold

shiver;
undulating
until the water stills
again

while it
stands, reflecting,
watching its own white
image.

C A M P

Light hikes
after sundown,
peering into thorny
thickets

along
a stony path,
finding tiny creatures
in the

bramble;
watching its own
startled shadows leap up
into

its beam;
singing a song
of bright flames around the
campfire.

SHADOWS

Light leans
against a door,
looks up to the shuttered windows

of old
buildings, searches
among the secrets of
shadows

and wood;
throws slanted
patterns across stone walls
and stands

transfixed,
puzzling on strange
objects reflected in
its gaze.

LATE AFTERNOON

Light rests
in the crooked
elbows and branches of
old trees,

drowses
in the shadows
of moss-covered rocks, naps
in piles

of leaves
scattered over
forest floors, stretches out
to sleep

and dreams
itself wearing
a shining necklace of
dewdrops.

FAMILY ROOM

Light hides
its face under
a lampshade, throwing strange
shadows.

against
the ceiling;
outlining the shapes of
tables

and chairs;
staring at the
changing, green-eyed numbers
of clocks

and the
flashing signals
and pictures jumbling on
TV.

2 A.M.

Light drifts
in the windows,
catching the gray leaves
stirring

in sleep;
throwing crazy
figures on the ceiling;
stretching

in blocks
across the walls;
bending slanted patterns
over

the doors,
and shimmering
silver pathways across
the floor.

The photographer thanks the following:

Philip Wood, tollmaster, Chesire Bridge, Charlestown, N.H., for "Toll Bridge"

Caesar's Pizza, Broadway at 17th Street, New York, New York, for "Diner"

Rikki Darter for "County Fair"

Evette Wenzel, M.D. for "Family Room"

Katrin Tchana, Michael O'Donnell, and John Quimby for back cover

The staff at The Camera Shop, Hanover, N.H.

Special gratitude to everyone at ProCam, White River Junction, Vt., for their patience and humor, particularly to Kathleen O'Donnell for her enormous skill

DATE DUE

MAY 3 1 1995			
GAYLORD			PRINTED IN U.S.A.